Reliable

A Cherrytree Book

Designed and produced by A S Publishing

First published 1996
by Cherrytree Press Ltd
327 High St
Slough
Berkshire SL1 1TX

First published in paperback 2002
Copyright this edition © Evans Brothers Limited 2002

British Library Cataloguing in Publication Data
Amos, Janine
    Reliable - (Viewpoints)
    1. Reliability - Juvenile literature 2. Moral development
    Juvenile literature
    I. Title
    155.4'1825

ISBN 1 84234 150 2

Printed in Spain by G. Z. Printek

VIEWPOINTS

Reliable

Two stories seen from
two points of view

by Janine Amos
Illustrated by Gwen Green

CHERRYTREE BOOKS

Laura and the sunflowers

There was a little patch of land outside Laura's door. In the spring she planted some sunflower seeds. She watered them every day and waited for them to grow.

"I want them to grow as high as the fence!" she said.

Soon there were several strong plants. Laura always checked them before she went to school. She made sure that there were no weeds. And she stopped her brother Tom from bouncing his football near the plants.

Laura's cousin Annie liked looking at the plants too. She helped Laura to water them sometimes.

"Who will look after them when you're on holiday?" asked Annie. "Let me do it," she begged. "Please!"

"OK," agreed Laura. "But you mustn't forget."

"I won't," promised Annie.

Laura and Tom had a great holiday. They sent postcards to all their friends.

"This one's for Annie," laughed Laura, holding up a card. It was a field full of sunflowers.

When they arrived home, Laura jumped out of the car. She couldn't wait to see her plants.

"I bet they're as tall as Tom now," she called.

But the sunflowers were all dried up. Their heavy heads were drooping on the ground.

Laura's eyes filled with tears. "They're dead!" she whispered, kicking at a lump of earth. "Annie let them die."

Read about Annie's side of things on page 16.

Jack and the school play

The hall was full of children, whispering and giggling. The class was starting work on the school play. Everyone was excited.

"I want to make scenery," said Rajan.

"I want to work the lights!" said Sarah.

Jack's eyes were shining. "I want to act," he told the others.

Just then, Mr Drew clapped his hands. "Volunteers, please," he said, "to try for the part of the Pied Piper."

Jack's hand shot up. So did Danny's.

"Remember," the teacher warned, "it's the main part. Whoever gets it will have to be here for every rehearsal – Mondays, Wednesdays and Fridays. And you'll need to help with the scenery, too."

Both boys nodded their heads. Jack could feel his heart thumping. He'd love to get that part.

Jack couldn't wait to get home with his good news.

"Yippee!" he shouted, as he burst through the door. "I'm the Pied Piper!"

"Great!" said his mum.

"Danny wanted the part, too," he told her. "But I got it."

"I expect you were the loudest!" joked Jack's sister Annie.

Jack raced to his room to try out his lines.

"Don't forget your music practice!" called his mum.

The first rehearsal was great fun. Mr Drew reminded everyone of the Pied Piper story. He showed them all where to stand for the opening scene. And he made them laugh by pretending to be a rat.

At the end of the rehearsal, Mr Drew called out, "Thanks everyone. See you all on Wednesday!"

"Wednesday is football training, " thought Jack. "I'll have to be late for rehearsal."

On Wednesday, Jack was first
in the shower after training. Soon
he was running to the hall. Everyone
was busy getting the stage ready.

"What happened to you?" whispered
Danny, as Jack crept in. "We've been
here for ages!"

Mr Drew came over. He gave Jack
a cross look. "Perhaps we can make a
start on some acting now?" he said.

The next day, Jack's music teacher told him off, too. He hadn't practised enough.

"You'll have to work harder if you want to stay in the orchestra," she said firmly.

Jack sighed.

From then on Jack was always in a hurry. He ran from football training to rehearsals. Then he ran home to do his music practice or learn his lines.

And there was never enough time to get everything done.

Jack was late for lots of rehearsals.

"We're sick of waiting for Jack!" grumbled Sarah.

"And he never helps out with painting the scenery!" Rajan complained.

"Everyone's picking on me," thought Jack.

Soon it was the very last rehearsal.

"Tomorrow the whole school will be watching us!" Mr Drew told the class. "Now's our last chance to get things right."

The scenery was nearly finished. The lights worked perfectly. Everything was going well. Then it was time for Jack's long speech. Halfway through, Jack stopped. He couldn't remember what came next!

"I never really learnt this bit!" Jack thought in a panic. He went bright red. Someone coughed.

The whole class started to mutter.

"It's not fair," said Sarah, "Jack's spoiling the play for everyone!"

"He's let us down," agreed Danny.

"Danny should have been the Piper!" said Rajan. "He's never late – and he knows all the words."

Jack felt terrible. "I can't help it!" he told them. "I've got too many things to do."

"That's not our fault!" said Danny.

Read about Danny's side of things on page 24.

15

Annie and the sunflowers

At first, looking after the sunflowers was fun Every evening after tea, Annie ran to Laura's house. She filled up the watering can from the outside tap. And she carefully poured the water along the row of plants. When she had finished, there was a dark patch of earth around each of them. Then she checked for snails under the leaves, just as Laura had shown her.

But one evening Annie forgot about the sunflowers. She had a new book to read. Then it was time for her bath.

When she was getting dry, she remembered the plants.

"Can I go and do them now?" she asked her mum.

"No!" said Annie's mum. "It's bedtime. You'll have to wait until tomorrow."

Annie was worried. "What if I forget again?" she asked.
"Write a note to remind yourself," suggested her mum.
Annie got out her crayons. She drew a big yellow
sunflower. Then she stuck the drawing on her bedroom door.
"I won't forget now!" said Annie as she climbed into bed.

The next day was very sunny.
When Annie got home from school
she was hot and tired.

"I'll go outside with a cold drink," she
thought.

First, Annie changed out of her school
clothes. She looked at the sunflower
picture on her bedroom door. And she
sighed.

"I'll do it later," thought Annie.

Annie sat outside in the sun. She thought about the sunflowers. They would be hot and thirsty too. But Annie didn't feel like walking to Laura's.

"I'll go tomorrow," she told herself.

The weather stayed hot. The next evening, Annie went for a picnic tea with her friend Meg.

Meg's house was quite near Laura's. Annie knew that she should go and water the plants. But she was having a good time.

"I can't go now, I'm playing with Meg," she thought.

On Saturday, Annie and her mum were out shopping.

"Laura and Tom will be back from their holiday," said Annie's mum. "Let's call in and see them on our way home."

"Oh no!" thought Annie. She hadn't been near the sunflowers for days. Annie felt a bit scared.

As soon as they got to Laura's house, Annie looked for the row of flowers. She saw the dried-up plants and she wanted to run home.

When Laura saw Annie she was cross.

"What happened to my flowers?" she shouted.

Annie went red.

"It wasn't my fault," she said. "It was too hot for them. And I was busy."

Danny and the school play

When he got home, Danny walked into the kitchen. He flopped down on to a chair. His mum looked at him.

"You didn't get the Piper part, then?" she asked.

"No," answered Danny. "Jack got it. I'm just the Mayor."

"Cheer up! That's a big part, too," said his mum. "You'll have to wear a cloak and a long, gold chain."

Danny liked the sound of that.

At the first rehearsal, Danny laughed a lot. Mr Drew had a great sense of humour. Danny decided to learn his lines as fast as he could.

On Wednesday, Danny was first to get to the hall. He jumped on to the stage and tried out his lines. He pretended that the hall was full of people.

Then the others arrived. Soon they were only waiting for Jack. Mr Drew kept looking up at the clock. But Jack still didn't come.

Everyone got bored with standing around. They started to talk.

"We'll do some work on the scenery while we wait," said Mr Drew, crossly.

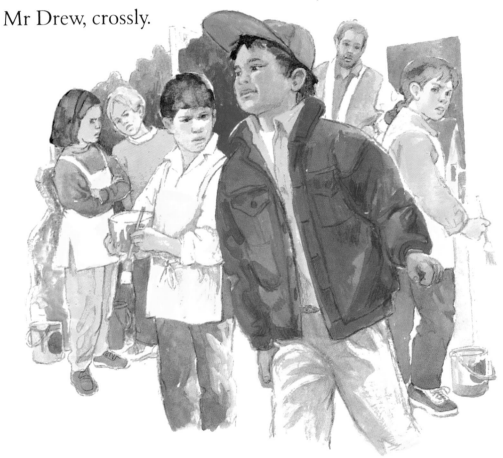

At last Jack came rushing in.
Danny didn't think he looked at all sorry.

On Friday there was more waiting. After a while, Mr Drew clapped his hands. "Right!" he said, frowning. "Let's start. We'll have to manage without Jack. I'll be the Piper for now."

Danny acted out his part. And Mr Drew pretended to be the Pied Piper. But he had to keep stopping to tell people what to do. It put Danny off.

"I'm fed up with this," he thought. "Why isn't Jack here?"

One afternoon, Mr Drew had some very exciting news. "Someone from the newspaper is coming to take our picture!" he told the class. "I'd like you all here tomorrow lunchtime – as soon as the bell goes."

The next day, everyone crowded into the hall and scrambled into their costumes. The photographer set up her camera. "I want a group scene, please – the Mayor, the Rats and, of course, the Pied Piper," she said.

"Where's Jack?" hissed Sarah. No one knew.

The photographer checked her watch. "I'll have to go ahead now," she told them.

Afterwards, Danny and the others talked about it.

"Trust Jack!" said Rajan.

"A photograph with the main person missing. It'll look stupid!" said Sarah loudly.

Then it was the last rehearsal. Danny stared around the hall in amazement. Everything looked so different! You could almost believe you were in a real town, long ago.

"We've done really well!" Danny told himself, proudly.

But then the spell was broken. Danny watched as Jack went red and stopped in the middle of his speech.

"Jack doesn't know his lines!" thought Danny. "All our hard work, and Jack will ruin it!"

Laura says

"It was Annie's fault. She says it was too hot and she was busy. Those are just excuses. I bet she didn't water my flowers once! She doesn't care. Annie's not reliable. Next time I'll ask someone else to look after my plants."

Annie says

"I meant to look after the sunflowers. I didn't want them to die. It's not fair to say I don't care. But I can see why Laura is cross. She was counting on me. Next time I make a promise I'll keep it. I'm sorry."

Danny says

"The play wasn't important to Jack. He couldn't be bothered to get to rehearsals on time. And he didn't care how long he kept us waiting. Jack's unreliable. You can't count on him. I don't think he should be in the next play."

Jack says

"The play was important to me. I tried hard to get to rehearsals on time and I hated being late. I wanted to do too many things, but there wasn't time and I didn't enjoy myself. From now on, I won't say yes to everything and I won't let people down."

BEING RELIABLE

Being reliable means doing what you say you will do. Everyone can learn to be reliable if they try. As Annie found, sometimes it can be hard to do what you've promised. Something more exciting may turn up, which you'd rather do instead. But remember how it feels to be let down. Thinking about other people's feelings makes it easier to keep your promises.

Jack learnt that it's difficult to be reliable if you take on too much. It's up to you to choose what you do – then stick to what you've agreed.

Everyone likes someone they can count on. Being reliable shows you care about others. And that's an important part of being a good friend.